The Cost
of Ambition

The Cost of Ambition

#1 Who Dreamt

Baibhav Agarwal

PARTRIDGE

To order additional copies of this book, contact
Partridge India
000 800 10062 62
orders.india@partridgepublishing.com

www.partridgepublishing.com/india

Contents

For mom, dad and my sister Juhi;

Thanks for everything.

1

Running and Hiding in The Struggling World

1992

At first, Atul felt that his heart was pounding against a bell metal, but when sleepiness gave way to consciousness, he realized that someone was banging the door, perhaps very violently. By the time he fully roused, a sense of nausea made him want to throw up. He was in a room with three basins which were adjacently placed to three cabins—a public toilet.

The other night was quite a run. Although he had succeeded to casually walk out of grocery shops and eating houses several other times, he couldn't get away from the owner last night. He had to run across alleys and passages, but when he felt a side stitch, all he could spontaneously resort to was hiding in a public toilet.

The past week had been like this over and over; it was like the night of the city always wanted to get into a brawl with Atul, but a new morning embraced him every day. This morning was no different; he opened the door of the public toilet, which he had locked the other night while trying to hide. He made his way through howls of men who waited for the door to open and walked back to . . . nowhere.

2

Contrasts Between Atul and His Village: The Birthplace of Contentment

1980

Dust and grime had become the breathing air of the village. The far end of the village itself looked like a construction site. Trucks carrying loads of coal went up and down every minute. Everyone knew that the land would be used for coal mining, and when people from the Sachdeva project came for a check, they knew that this place was going to be a living filth. Mining brought about a number of drawbacks and danger with itself, but when little Atul saw the gigantic vehicles coming in and out of the village, his heart throbbed at the look of them. He went running to his father at his grocery store.

'Papa, can I work at the mining site?'

Kumarji laughed. 'But, *beta*, you will hurt yourself if you go near those huge mining machineries. Then who will turn my grocery store into a big market?'

Atul's child heart instantly got burdened with responsibility, and it almost sank at the thought of sitting in a market.

1984

Years passed by, and by the time Atul reached his early teens, school had become an upsetting place, where whatever the *masterji* spoke went above his head. Other children seemed strange to Atul. Boys were always fighting, and girls were always playing. Even though Atul tried hard to study, he couldn't. It was unfair for him because everyone knew how much of a bright kid he was. He himself felt enclosed, like he was strangled to a rag through which he might never breathe out.

It would not be possible to know the feeling of suffocation when someone had never stepped out in a different environment. When one could see the same process taking place around, one would think that it was the only normal way of living. That was the state of the people in the village. They never saw what life outside the village was, and anything that looked alien to their way of living were ignored because, after all, ignorance was bliss—but not to Atul.

Atul had an eye for everything that people who were older than him could do. It was because when a classmate at school punched Atul on his nose, he lost the power of reasoning. He knew it very well that a grown-up man wouldn't punch him down if he tried to reason it out with him for anything.

And then the situation at home never seemed to get fixed; his mother would go on about the miseries of life. What else could that poor soul do in a house that started and ended in twenty steps? She was not cranky by nature, but the Fates took over her understanding of life.

Years passed by, and she never saw a silver lining. Whatever Kumarji could earn out of a grocery shop was only enough to survive on food. There was absolutely no penny left for what she could do to have a happy moment to herself. Marriage means so much beyond the happiness of two. Not that she had a doubt about how Kumarji would turn out to be, but financial satisfaction was so important.

So this was how everything looked like around Atul's life. In the village, the people were more than content with themselves. There was no hope of him gelling with his schoolmates. Teachers couldn't get over books, and so life learning eventually came from nowhere.

Kumarji was different. He completed his schooling in his village. But life after completing school became difficult. There was no means by which Kumarji could move any further. After his father died, everything that was left behind by him was taken away by Kumarji's brothers; they left their old mother behind with Kumarji. He had no way out but to start with anything that came at his doorstep so as to take care of his mother. When he got married, people thought that they'd be well off because the grocery store brought in a good amount of money. But within the year, more shops were set up and less money flew in and now a total of three people were living under one compact roof.

When the old mother passed away, Atul then came in. Struggles for Kumarji were never-ending. It was too late for him to leave his grocery store. What would have been easy was to make money and run away to a better life while he was still young. But there was something that his heart was made up of; he was a man so optimistic and could never do wrong. That was the reason he kept his mum even when his very friends started to cause harm by spreading news about acts of duplicity going on in his grocery store.

These incidents did tremble Kumarji's virtuous self. When a buyer came out in the village to announce about fragments of bricks and stones found in the rice, Kumarji ran to his shop to check not only the rice but other commodities. What if he was being fooled by the distributors? But all the tins were clean, with only the right commodity in it.

Atul silently saw everything that his father went through. Somehow, he was always aware of the hardships of his father's life, but there was no doubt that he would do anything for the happiness of Atul, and that was the reason Atul wanted to give back a lot to Kumarji.

For a few years in his early teens, fourteen-year-old Atul kept himself from telling his parents that he made money at the mining site. He just couldn't keep himself from that place. When the elder ones told him 'Mining brings you a lot of money', he was thrilled by the idea of contributing in the project and, in return, take back a lot for himself.

It all started when a younger Atul stood beside Mishraji, the local head, and observed every activity that Mishraji would involve himself in. Mishraji was a stout, wheatish, half-bald man who had his way with workers. He knew just what vague reason the workers would give so as to get away from work for some time. He scolded them in a way that they would silently walk back to the site.

Not that Mishraji never noticed this young boy beside his table who was speculating in a way as if he was on patrol. In fact, Mishraji was always amused when he saw the boy running from afar in his school uniform, a rectangular bag pulled down from his hand so as to take its burden while running, facing downwards. Some days when Atul failed to turn up, Mishraji would look out for him in the entire field but instantly forget about it when work would come up.

After a year and a few more months passed, Atul had reached a typical kind of pubescence. His skin was transitioning from that of a child to that of a teenager. Due to this, there was a shift from a fair skin to a more of a light olive with a yellow undertone. One might say that he was fully grown because of his tall figure of five feet and eleven inches, but when he was looked at closely, his facial hair and the little 'dirt' on his upper lips would say something different. He smelled funny, but his extremely descriptive features were irresistible. Those eyes had the colours of grey and brown all at once. The eyebrows had that sharp arc that seemed like they were carved with the help of a sword.

More than his physical features, there was an energy that he emitted which was extremely youthful and controlling. When it was his turn to hit the selected *goti*, other boys sweated internally, but a portrayal of mockery was well performed from the outside. This time, for the eleventh time in a row, Atul was going to hit an aim which would touch the right place. He was going to, yet again, strike this tough play. These *goti* games fetched him money to get two *samosas* for himself every day. He was not selfish, but he liked the fact that he ate from his own money. It also meant that money for his share of food would not have to be shelled out from his father's earnings.

It was the day when class 11's exams got over, and it was also the day when Atul was going to make some decisions that would change his life for good. The wait was over.

Fed up with school, he still waited to grow old and get some wise learning from this institution.

'Now I'll know schooling did good to me, now, now, now.' But 'now' never seemed to cross his path. Frustration took over.

How long will Father even wait for me? he thought to himself.

Defeat is not when you fall down; its
when you refuse to get up.

3

Earning in The First Set of Years

Mishraji saw Atul running towards him. He winded up his books and got himself ready to talk to Atul. He had been waiting for the correct moment to speak to him. He knew that his exams were over, so it was the correct time to talk to him. He set up a chair for him and Atul to sit on. Then Atul arrived.

'Come sit, Atul.'

'Mishraji, I want to talk to you . . .'

'Me too. Come sit, take a breath.'

Atul couldn't get his head around why Mishraji was being so welcoming. He didn't want to be an entertainer for one of Mishraji's storytelling today. He couldn't wait to spill out his thoughts.

But then Mishraji spilled out too, 'Come work for me, young man.'

Atul was taken aback. 'What?'

'Why not? I'm not asking you to pick up coals for me.'

'No, no. I meant—actually, I myself came running to you to talk about the same thing, Mishraji.'

Mishraji smiled and exclaimed, 'So how about starting with handling petty accounts?'

1988

One year passed, and the village looked the same, if not even more of a mining site. The workers were working efficiently, and the excavation as well as transportation of coal were going in a good pace. Mishraji had got older and weaker or, so to speak, lazy. He couldn't handle the daily commotion of workers and keep checking on the money outflow at the same time. But he did not have much to worry about.

Atul, with time, had become more talented. When he went in the mining site, he was made responsible to give away daily wages to the workers. But he couldn't keep himself ignorant when he came to know that there was a minor discrepancy between the number of workers and the amount of wages going out. He instantly went to Mishraji along with a possible solution in the head. From the next day onwards, there was a log maintained against which the workers got their midday meals.

There were many other changes he brought in—from setting up a kitchen to bringing about electricity savings, all of which showed quite a difference in the expenses sheet of Mishraji with 100 per cent working efficiency.

It was now time for Kunal Sachdeva to visit for a check. Last time he came in, there was not much hope with the way things were working at the site. This time around, Mishraji's excitement went over the head. He laid his eyes far away to the end of the site and the road through which trucks passed by. It was a clear day, and everyone looked engrossed in their work. Other times, Mishraji would get lethargic on the visit of Kunal Sachdeva. Both sides knew that there was not much they could improve in the working manner of the mining site.

To be honest, Kunal Sachdeva himself did not show much enthusiasm towards bringing about good working conditions in the village. He would stride in to the mining site in a brown suit (yes, it had been nothing else

4

Meeting The Master

Kunal Sachdeva stepped out of the car as his driver held out the door for him; he was a fair tall man with a face of ambition and wealth. Those precision cheekbones looked enhanced by perfectly fit round black sunglasses. But the brown on his suit—that brown looked a shade brighter to Mishraji today. He knew it was a going to be a good day.

Atul was bedazzled. He'd watched such men of charisma only in movies, which he went to once in every two weeks at the Kalpana Cinema. Kunal Sachdeva was a handsome man, with his hair combed to perfection and clothes ironed to stark plain. His watch told the same time as the others but was worth fifty of them bought together. His flat black leather shoes still shone from in between the smut from the village land.

After noticing all this, Atul noticed himself: a clay-toned boy with a grotty face; messy hair; bare, dusty hands; half-sleeved rosewood-and-brown checked shirt; ash pants which were picked up from the mess on the floor; a pair of black rubber slip-ons on his feet. As much as Atul felt sorrowful, he was also excited by the gleaming look of Kunal Sachdeva. After all these years, now he knew what the villagers meant when they said, 'Mining brings you a lot of money.'

Atul waited for the day to arrive when the big people will come down for an inspection at the mining site and approve all the better changes that took place due to him. That day had finally come. He had a feeling that if the changes came across as fitting, then it would turn out to be his accomplishment. Not only that; he might get a higher post among the decision makers of the mining site.

In the searing heat of the day, Kunal Sachdeva stood afresh under the shadow of the umbrella which was held out for him by a fellow worker. Atul couldn't imagine wearing a suit in that heat, but he wondered and got stuck at the thought of how fine he would look if he put on one of those.

'Mishraji, what is this news that has been flying into my ears?'

Sweaty Mishraji only became clammier. 'Has there been a mistake, Malik?'

Sachdeva broke into fits. They could see he enjoyed all the torture that he could make people go through by just a remark that he made.

'*Arrey*, Mishraji! *Kya aap bhi*? You should be happy. Did you feed yourself with some sweets or not?'

Atul jumped.

Sachdeva's eyes laid on the chap. 'You better be Atul and not some random fellow of the village.'

'Yes, sir.' Not a word more. He already slapped himself in his mind for jumping in front of Sachdeva like a maniac.

'Yes, you are a random fellow?'

'No, sir.'

'Oh! So you consider yourself very supreme, I see.'

'No, sir.'

'Do you speak more than *yes*, *no*, and *sir*?'

'I am Atul. I help Mishraji in setting up facilities at the mining site.'

Sachdeva took his glasses off and placed it on his forehead to look into those eyes whose colour one could never tell. Brown or grey? He couldn't tell the colour but could surely find vivacity in them.

5

This Will Change Everything

Everyone went back to their homes as the evening arrived. Atul was distressed by the short encounter that he had with the man himself. His intentions were to shine through the crowd, beaming with his confidence, but nothing went according to the plan. He tried getting some sleep, only to lose it. Distress took over completely, and Atul only hoped the morning to arrive, which would decide the making or breaking of so many situations and circumstances in his and his family's life. He was wide awake when the morning arrived in front of his eyes.

In the *makaan* of Sachdeva, he was getting ready for the day. He had some important things to deal with. This village had started with the project in front of Sachdeva. He used to go along with his father to inspect the sight and was very apt with every work which was parted to him. When the father died, Kunal had to take over the entire workload all at once, which was daunting as well as heartening at the same time. But he couldn't do much about the happiness of the workers. His father had personal touch with all the sites and their workers, but nothing was officially maintained that would ensure continuity with the prosperity of workers. So when Kunal took over, he couldn't bring about welfare to these people.

And then he was ambitious—overly at times. The feeling of power gave him so much satisfaction that most of the time he would drown in intimidation and dominance. But one day it struck him while looking at his father's picture. How was he equally good as his father? He was reaching his old age, and it scared him that he'd be dead one day and would not be remembered for good.

When this particular village brought news of the advancement of amenities, due to which the work was also affected in a positive way, Kunal saw a ray of light. He communicated with Mishraji and, as time suited best, visited their mining site. And now that he was here, Kunal had lined up the same plans to be executed in other mining sites. He wanted to uplift the working conditions, and all of a sudden, he looked beyond just his selfish reasons of reputation to do so and also foresaw the overall betterment of workers, their efficiency, and furthermore, his business in the industry.

Seeing Atul, well, he had some plans for him, which he hoped would take place.

6

When The City Calls, You Got to Go

At the mining site, Atul was checking some previous calculations from the register when Kunal Sachdeva walked in. His all-time sharp looks adding to the husky voice could give cold sweats to anyone. 'Show me the financial recordings you have maintained in the past six months.'

Atul put a scale in the page he went through last, got up, and walked to the small outside cabin that they recently got made to maintain all the private and important books, receipts, files, and other papers. Sachdeva went around with him to the cabin, and as Atul unlocked the door, he stood at the threshold, startled.

Atul stopped and turned. 'Sir, please come and sit here. We have maintained historical books of five years.'

Sachdeva only saw this type of maintenance at his office in the city. What he had in front of his eyes was neat and clearly mentioned sections of shelves that were labelled according to year and subdivided with types of papers.

He had left nagging with the local heads of the sites about maintaining records; if they had to do it, they would. Later on, Kunal Sachdeva was unsure if this is how things would work out. His employees at work, none of them were capable enough to handle the on-ground check of these mining sites because they were so used to office space. So eventually, the situation was falling out of Kunal Sachdeva's control.

'How long did you take to divide and subdivide all of this?'

'We took roughly thirty days to sort this. We also tried to get together all the papers from before I joined. That should be 1988, so we managed to bring together the papers from 1984 onwards.'

Atul then took Kunal Sachdeva for a tour to and around the site—sheds, hospitals, generator room, and electricity rooms, and inside the excavation route, where workers were operating machineries and digging out. Everything looked like a massive manoeuvre; everything looked like a panorama from the time of Kunal Sachdeva's father, even better.

Atul showed diligence in showing him around and catering to the interrogations, as well as clearing all the doubts, although, inside his heart, he almost craved to be impressive.

They had long discussions where Kunal Sachdeva did not miss even a single opportunity to know all the corners of Atul's brains. 'At the end of the day, he was just a young fellow who did not even pursue proper education. On the contrary, all of Kunal Sachdeva's employees are well educated.' Sachdeva snapped out of his thoughts. He had to know exactly why Atul couldn't complete his schooling. He was pretty confident that they would conclude Atul submitting himself to the weakest link and Kunal would think that he only wasted his time on a laddie.

Sachdeva's perception took a turn when he heard Atul's story, while the villagers who passed by were only at awe because they never saw Sachdeva speaking so much to someone and that too with Atul.

Atul might just be a massive contributor to the mining site, but to the villagers, Atul was an overconfident lad. Maybe deep inside, they did know that Atul had a charm about himself, but how could they admit that? They saw their own children of the same age, or even older, struggling with school and making money for the house. Talks were that Atul brought in a wad of money to his parents. The villagers stayed in denial.

Sachdeva was a very well-read man. He completed his schooling as a top ranker and was a very proficient student during his college days, always focussed about academics, knowing that it could bring a lot of advantages to his career in taking forward his father's business. But when Atul spoke about the odd nature of the institution of academics, Sachdeva was rather in shock. He could not imagine himself daring questioning an institution which had been standing and nurturing great men of this world; although sometimes in his student life he did contemplate on the existence of the whole system, he never took the thought so seriously. He could not even deny that his educational life brought in a lot of changes to his way of thinking and personality.

Just to hear someone think otherwise—and not just think it but also make a big decision on that thought— was very interesting to Sachdeva. This could mean a lot. He was instantly impressed.

'Toh Atul, kal mai tumhare ghar chai par aa raha hu.'

Atul looked up to the neat face from the ground that he was sitting on. He sat there, perplexed. At this very moment, he felt gutted because now Sachdeva was taking too much interest in him and had not even spoken a word to leave a hint here and there.

'How about you come to the city with me?'

'What?'

All this while, Sachdeva didn't leave any hints, and now he dropped the bomb all at once.

'Yes, you should come to the office with me and work there.' No look of welcome showed on Sachdeva's face. He never showed it.

By now, Atul's mouth had remained opened, and he was still wide-eyed. There was a flash of possible moments in front of him. Until only a few minutes back, he was hoping to get a place in the higher management of the mining site, but Sachdeva had broken that board of expectation and placed a new shelf altogether, a shelf in which Atul would rearrange his life afresh. He went through images of his home, his parents, his clothes, the food . . .

'Arrey, kaha kho gaye?'

Atul dreamt like a thirteen-year-old again. But Sachdeva pulled him back with an uptight attitude.

'Go, now.' It was as if Sachdeva took it as a yes even if Atul didn't respond. 'Go home, and I'll see you for tea tomorrow morning.'

Atul was still silent. He was overwhelmed, but as he stood up and turned back to walk towards his house, it struck him that he had forgotten to take one person in his flash of pictures.

7

Wait, Isn't There Always A Lover?

At 11 p.m., it was like midnight for this village. The roads were empty as a dessert. The orange streetlights were lit alternatively, making the lanes look like a picture of dimness. The sleek, cool breeze blew all across; no one could tell that the mornings were searing and scorching. In a shabby flat of two walk-ups, the glass pane of the upper floor was faintly creaking as if a pigeon flew in again and again to just touch its beak to the glass and then flew back and around. On the other side of the window, in the room, Simran was sleeping, and when she was just going to drown in a deeper sleep, it was like the pigeon hit the glass with its beak real hard this time.

Simran woke up startled, took a broom in her hand, irritated, and opened the window to see a boy standing outside the flat, looking up, about to throw another pebble at the window.

'*Aehhh!*'

'Simran!'

'Atul? It is eleven o'clock at night. What is so important that you were ready to put your life at stake? If *Baba* comes . . .'

'Ssshh. If you'll speak so much, your *Baba* will definitely wake up to find me and then murder me.'

'So why are you here? Go back, and we'll see each other after my school in the lane of the back gate.'

Atul was suddenly stunned by the look of Simran. Her long black locks of hair flung out from the window, and Atul noticed for the first time that her hair was that long. She was a face of the moon. The little spots on her face didn't obstruct the beaming face that she possessed. Her eyes were so black that one could differentiate them from the light that her skin emitted.

'Did you go deaf, silly boy?' Simran squeaked.

Atul was pulled back.

'Go! I said I'll see you tomorrow.'

'Okay, but you better see me surely.' Atul said as if commanding.

Simran took a second to read him, then dropped it, and closed back the curtains.

Who is an entrepreneur? Someone who jumps off a cliff and builds a plane on the way down.

8

Bashed Up By Life: Reflecting Part I

1992

Atul walked up to the fifth floor of the building and reached the apartment, but before entering, he stood in front of the closed door; eyes squeezed shut. His mind was telling him, 'Just another day. One more week, and you'll not have to face the shamefulness again.'

He knocked at the green door. A boy of his age opened the door and almost swung his head right and left as he gave way for Atul to enter. This has been a continuous process for a week. When Atul had come to the city back again, he had no place to stay, but he knew this guy from Sachdeva's office who apparently would let him stay for a few days until he gets a job. But not even a week had passed by, and the guy from office had started to show agitation towards Atul's presence in his apartment. Atul had enough ego to move out of the apartment immediately and only requested him to keep his luggage. He'd come back in the mornings to clean himself and change his clothes. Atul did not mention where he would manage to sleep during the nights, nor did the guy from the office asked.

Atul went straight into the room to open his suitcase and take out fresh clothes. He took a quick bath and came out.

A standing mirror in the room showed a lean man in a towel. His sex hormones were effective; he got back his fair skin with a yellow undertone. But his physique had passed through leanness and then anorexia. His eyes were small and wide, but the skin underneath had become saggy. His hands had a distinctive tan on them from the half shirts he wore during the burning daytime in the city. His stomach was a slab of bone, and those legs looked as if they were pieces of bamboo.

But nothing underneath would show once he dressed himself neat and tidy. And the physical pain, the emotional ache in his heart, well, that would get hidden by the youthful enthusiastic face he was now used to putting up. And no, he was not used to putting up this particular look since his time in the city. He'd kept up that look since childhood. He'd always had rough days, but all he knew was that everyone wanted to take a positive, dauntless, and energetic face.

He put on a bottle-green shirt and ash trousers; these pants reminded him of the pants he once owned when he saw Kunal Sachdeva for the first time. He chuckled at the relevance and went on to start his day.

This was not the first time Atul had seen the city. He knew the streets and bus routes of this area very well. In this very area, he had once worked at Sachdeva projects.

Now that he thought of it, taking the decision of going to the city with Sachdeva was a turning point in his young life. The morning tea with Sachdeva back at the village had gone very well; Atul's mother shed a few tears but did not grieve at the thought of her son going away because she knew that this would change many unattended situations in the lives of all three in the Kumar family. Kumarji was proud; he always thought highly of Kunal Sachdeva, and to know that his son would work under the shadow of this well-bred man, Kumarji was content.

There was nothing left for Atul in that village anyway. He was growing up, and if at that moment he wouldn't taste an ideal life, then it would be too late for him; moreover, Kumarji was concerned that even Atul would become too comfortable to step out of his zone so as to see larger things in life.

As for Simran, she was too young to react in a positive way. She was at that stage of growing up where she thought Atul was her own possession and would not take it well if someone or something tried to take him away from her. Atul left it there with Simran but said he would come back for her to take her to the city.

He did go back. He was thrown out of the office, accused of irresponsibility.

Kunal Sachdeva shook his head. He knew that Atul might not have had his hands in the wrongdoing, but he was mostly unpleased by the way a petty situation turned out to be a big fuss. In the village, he might have had a lot of spare time to be the ears to an entire misguided situation, and that was how Atul thought Sachdeva to be.

But back in the city, Kunal Sachdeva was an inconsiderate man. He was this cold being on his extravagant seat in his enclosed office. It was like that the door was there only for a formality because the boss never liked anyone inside of his chamber.

At Atul's first attempt of whining, Sachdeva's reflex was to call for security.

Atul was later told in an unofficial meeting with Sachdeva's assistant that the boss was aware of the ill behaviour of his employees but Atul's immature way of handling a minor situation was entirely unnecessary. When Atul asked why he was not given a chance to brush himself back again, the assistant said, 'You don't get second chances in a top-most company.'

Atul remained silent.

The assistant loosened up and went further. 'Look, Atul, I myself come from a weak background, and I understand how left out and hopeless you must be feeling at the moment.'

Hopeless, Atul thought to himself. 'Yes, that is exactly how I feel.'

The assistant continued, 'It is just that I have always witnessed Sachdeva sir as a cold man. You must have had a different notion about this man, which he is not—or at least, he does not get time to be that. I had my ways with dealing controversial situations because, honestly, I was myself involved in the cause of many office controversies. That's how people are at big places. Even they are struggling to make the same money that you are desperate of making, and believe me, everyone would go to any extent to be at a better place.'

'Even if it is about making someone lose their job?'

'Deep inside, maybe that is not their intention. Maybe that night they went to sleep with a feeling of guilt, but they have become very strong.'

'Not strong, but hard—as a rock.'

'Maybe, yes, they have. But their job is secure. Not yours. See, Atul, you have been around good people who do not show bad intentions in their actions. Here, people are all out with their actions. It is better you go back to the village and work at the mining site. You were good at it without any competition. I'll talk to Sachdeva sir, and he'll take care of your travelling expenses.'

9

Fright For How Life Would Look Like: Reflecting Part II

Daytime in the village was the time of knock-back for Atul. He withheld himself inside the house. His mother asked him to go out and meet his 'friends'. There was no one for him out there. He never made any friends! Kumarji asked him to rejoin the mining site, but he wouldn't listen.

He wouldn't go out in the open so as to be jeered at, laughed at. Moreover, meeting the people at the mining site would mean bringing up the topic, which was put to silence by Atul, and then talking about it would look like giving an explanation, which would eventually make him regretful, like he had wasted time, energy, and hard work. Then he'd have to tackle the laments of how they were harrowed about the whole circumstance.

What about the people who despised him silently? They'd get another chance to announce their unworthy preaching: 'People stay where they belong.' But Atul, he never belonged here. He belonged to something extravagant, something unrestrained. Then what happened?

The nights were like a beast that was wide awake, glaring back at Atul, scorning, standing over him. 'You will be good here *without any competition.*'

The very thought of spending his life in one place, in this place, scared him. At some evenings, Simran would request for him to see her, and they would meet by the pond.

'I can't stay here any more, Simran.'

Simran was minutely hurt to know about Atul's way of thinking at that moment, but she knew that what he wanted was what he wanted really badly. She had seen him running all around the site just to make a tiny bit of glitch work out. With time, she had shrugged off adolescence from her shoulders, and now she had her own life too. She had passed school, and now it was time for her to take an undergraduate course. Even then, in spite of a shift in her life, she did feel a pinch when Atul said he wanted to get away from everything.

To Atul, Simran was the only one with whom he could speak to. She would not go against his opinions, and that settled his mind for good. It was like he could talk to himself when he spoke out to Simran. It was like he was telling himself more than telling her.

Then the day came when he heard himself while talking to Simran. He heard himself. He wanted to go back and work in a different, much-low-scale company. He had his set of skills, and they would be fit for some job or other. He barely had knowledge about posts in an office, but if he got to the city, he was sure to grab something from anywhere and everywhere.

He decided to leave for the city within a week. There was absolutely no preparation for what he was going to do in the city, but he was positive.

'I suggest you should work here and simultaneously get knowledge about what you could do in the city. It is not a fair deal to go there directly without a sketched plan.' Kumarji spoke for the first time.

'No, Papa. I am going to go there, and I am sure, I'll be able to work anything out, whatever comes my way.'

At this point, Kumarji caught a look on Atul's face which told him that Atul was now taking his capabilities for granted. But he was not sure. At this point, in fact, he was not sure what kind of father to be. He couldn't figure out what to suggest and how to control the situation.

He let it be. Once Atul reached the city, they would automatically come to know how everything would eventually look like.

Yes, Atul should have listened to Kumarji. But this was only a side thought in his head. Atul was taken aback by the first jolt of getting kicked out from various offices. He did not take it well for the first time. Initially, he thought that if he was brought into the city by a big man like Sachdeva to work in his office, then he could easily start a new job anywhere mediocre.

'Whatever consequences happened later on was another story altogether,' he told himself.

The truth was, Atul knew he had to learn more than he already knew. What scared him was that he didn't know how to. This feeling strangled him even more, and so, in order to help himself through, he wanted to be out there. 'It can be the only way to learn. To see it, to go through it, can be the only way to learn.'

Upon all this, of course, he had resorted to many ways of surviving in the city which he never thought he would have to take up. Back in the village, he would earn for his own share of food, but here he walked in and out of places without paying—until the other day when one of the staff of a store caught him leaving without making a payment and ran after him with three more fellows.

Atul's heart was pounding. It struck him only then that he had been unknowingly committing a crime. In a flash, he saw himself running for the next thirty or more years of his life. Sitting in the public toilet, his imaginations started to wander to different corners, and it felt like he would never earn money, never be able to get food for himself and his parents, never wear good clothes, and never splurge on things he liked: a house with finest of furniture, a vehicle, a rack of ties, a pair of filthy expensive sunglasses, watches, and suits in more colours than just brown. His father would never taste richness, and his mother would never make it out of the village to make trips and shop all she wanted.

He was mournful.

Everything broke down, shattering above him. He buried his face in both his palms while sitting on the white tiles of a public toilet. He saw Simran, her widening smile, and her black eyes. He would never be able to make a future with Simran. Why would her *Baba* give her away to someone who didn't have anything to himself?

But he recalled the optimism of Simran. She wanted him to have a run for everything he dreamt of. Atul's mind calmed down, and it gave way to sleep.

10

The City Called Again,
You Got To, Got To Go

The nights were a brawl. The mornings embraced. This morning had its arms wide open.

On the newspaper was a job posting from PCM & Co. Why Atul's interest went to this particular posting in the heap of many others was just because this did not have any information. The other ones clearly mentioned who they were looking for: a teacher, a salesman, a model.

So when Atul came across PCM & Co., he rang the given contact number then and there to find out where the office was.

He looked up to the hustle and bustle of the road; men and women in their clean, sharp clothes were walking, travelling, pushing through to get to work. There was a flickering light of hope for him today. At least, he had something to look forward to; maybe this was going to be *the* workplace. Maybe this was where he would make his first set of money.

He couldn't wait for the clock to strike three. Restlessness had taken over. Now that his imaginations started to work, he couldn't wait to know what PCM & Co. was all about. The more he built it up on his imagination, the more disappointed he might just get—or fortunate.

He decided to go to PCM & Co. anyway. He took a bus and reached the nearest bus stop. He stopped to check himself in the reflection of a glass window of a bank's ATM and then saw a woman standing inside to take out some money and immediately shrugged at it.

Moving forward, he was half-looking up and half-looking ahead while walking. *503 . . . 504 . . . 506 . . . 506/1 . . . there!* It was a sober-looking, white-painted building which seemed like a five-storey building, a wide one because it had one entrance each for two different complexes. Atul didn't know which one to get into. He entered the first entrance and found no one. This building had no letter box to determine if PCM & Co. was in this side of the building, so he went outside and walked to the second entrance. Here he found letter boxes but couldn't find the name of the company.

He also caught hold of the watchman and asked him where PCM & Co. was. The watchman ignorantly pointed out to his left direction.

Atul raised his eyebrows. 'Heh?'

The watchman rolled his eyes and spoke, 'It's in the other building.'

'Well, why is there no watchman there, and why are there no letter boxes or any list which tells which floor has what and whom?'

The watchman bent forward towards Atul, and this time, he raised his brows. 'Are you Santosh sir's son?'

'What? No! I am here to visit PCM & Co.'

'So go ahead. Don't waste your time and mine.' The watchman put his shoulders at the back of his head and sat back on his chair.

Atul was only wasting his time, so he walked outside to enter the first entrance again. This time, he found a boy sitting on a chair.

'Which floor is PCM & Co.?' Atul asked.

'Up. Second floor,' the watchman replied.

Atul felt like he could have a chat with this boy. *'Acha ek baat batao . . .'* He digressed for a second. 'What's your name?'

'Shankar,' the boy replied.

'Okay, Shankar, tell me something. What does PCM & Co. do?'

'They work *na*. They have an office on second floor. Everyone comes in shirt and—'

Atul snapped, 'Yes, yes. They have an office. But what do they work on?'

'Oh! Plastic bottles. They are a plastic-bottle manufacturer.'

Atul paused to think about it. *Plastic-bottle manufacturer . . .* Then he swallowed it and grinned at this boy whose name Atul now knew as Shankar.

'Yes, they are the grimmest set of people,' Shankar continued.

Atul was surprised. He did not see that hitting message coming. 'Why?' He chuckled. 'Why would you say that?'

Shankar sniggered. 'Because they are never bright or welcoming. They never talk or put up a good face. At first, it unsettled me a little, but later, on one of those days when I was chilling with the peon of the office, I came to know that they are going through a very tough time.'

'Really?' This did not put Atul in dismay. He wanted to know more.

'*Bhaiya*, I do not understand much, but they are having a time of struggle with the bank. The people from the bank have visited them twice in front of me. I also heard that they are going to shut down soon and a new ladies' parlour will open here.' Shankar, by now, looked like as if someone put a hanger in his mouth.

Atul disapproved instantly, and Shankar's illusions were shattered then and there.

Atul came out on the street for a while. There was still some time left for the clock to strike three. Until then, he made up his mind. He was going to walk in and understand the scenario completely. He had done it before—bringing about good working conditions. Yes, he had.

'How bad would it be?' Atul assured himself.

It was five minutes to 3 p.m. Atul walked up to the second floor; it was an empty floor with two doors opposite to each other. From the look of one of the doors, it seemed like it was already desolated because it had a lock on its grille with noticeable cobwebs and dust on it.

The door opposite to it was a reed-glass door that had a Sunmica boundary which looked close to a pale yellow. Behind this door was the office of PCM & Co.

Unconsciously, Atul took a minute to agonize over his struggle till date. A whoosh of moments ran through where Atul toiled from dropping school to working at the mining site, to hoping for something better from life and being picked up by Sachdeva, and to being scorned at and still coming back here, only to face rejections.

Atul knew that there was a missing part to his way of handling the situations in life. He felt it from the inside that he was still to feel something correct strike somewhere correct. He was immature. That was a sad truth. He was immature, and maybe he did take a stand which came out of his foolishness. But he was ready; he was ready to be slapped at. He was ready to learn the unlearned. He was ready to unlearn and learn again.

So he pushed through the door with a lot of zest, only to snap himself out of it.

11

Silver Linings

The melancholia from outside of the door loomed back in. This place had a thick air, and the room was stifling. A woman who sat right in front of the door looked up with her eyes of doziness. 'Yes?'

Atul pulled himself back. 'I was over the phone with you this morning. I have come here for the job posting you made in the newspaper?'

'Oh! You have come for that job posting,' the woman said with her dozy eyes widening.

'Yes, is there a problem?'

'No, Nandi sir will see you in a mi—'

Before she could complete it, a man broke in, hurriedly saying rather rudely, 'Yes? What are you here for?'

'Nandi sir, this boy has come from the reference of the newspaper's job posting.' The woman informed the man, who now had a name—Nandi sir.

Dev Nandi was the boss at PCM & Co. He was a fair-skinned, healthy-looking man at 5.9 inches, with a distinctive peroxide-blonde hair. His face looked like he bore a lot of tension and that he had nobody to share his worries with. Dev Nandi was going to decide a lot of things for Atul.

Atul put his hand forward for a handshake, and Dev Nandi's mouth remained open while he mechanically did a handshake with Atul. 'Hello, Mr Nandi. I am Atul Kumar. Nice to meet you.'

'Yes. Wait in my cabin. I'll be there in a minute.'

Atul walked straight into a cabin, quickly running through as many things as he could in his sight. It was a long office with dull light-green walls; it had almost a dozen cubicles in one stretch of two on each side, and employees sitting there were . . . doing nothing.

How bad could it be? Atul kept telling himself.

Outside in the hallway, Dev Nandi asked the woman in a compressed tone, 'What is this young boy doing here?

Did you not ask him anything or took information from him before calling him in?'

'No, he sounded like a grown-up,' the woman responded in a very uninformed fashion.

Annoyed, Nandi hissed at her furiously, 'Well, I don't pay you to just attend calls or to waste my time and to waste other people's time.' And he strode back into his cabin.

'So Atul Kumar, is that right?' Nandi asked Atul while entering his cabin and going around Atul and the desk to reach to his seat.

'Yes, sir.'

'Please.' Nandi offered him a glass of water with a sign of his hands. 'So, Atul, I can see there has been miscommunication. We are looking for men more developed in their age to handle work here. Apparently, that was supposed to be communicated to you over the phone call. But obviously, there has been a discrepancy.'

Atul remained silent.

'See, child, you may ask me anything you want. You can take my time because we have taken yours. But to give you a heads-up, we have nothing to give you here.'

Atul tried to space his words in the hopeless situation. 'But, sir, I can be of help to your office work.'

Nandi hesitated. 'Right, you see, we have a lot of people here working already. Look, if we have anything in the future to offer, we will. But as much as I hate to say it, at the moment, we have got nothing at all.'

'Well, if you have so many people working, then what is going wrong with your firm?' Atul took a long shot.

Nandi was put in a state of shock. 'Excuse me?'

'I have heard about your firm. You are not well off currently. What is it? Not enough clients? The bank's pressurising you a lot?'

Nandi chuckled. 'Yeah, right. Kid, I don't think you're in the right territory.'

'Well, why not? Look, I've done these types of problem-solving for most of my life.'

'How old are you, twelve?'

'Entering twenty-one. And try me!'

'Go ahead.'

Atul stunned Nandi with his working history. But Nandi didn't put any look on his face.

For Atul, well, for him, it was a revelation of its own. He never knew his skills aptly until the time he was left feeling gutted. Atul's life events were all about solving problems—not just at work, but also at home. Or with the way he wanted to handle his future, all he was doing was solving problems.

Gradually and while speaking, Atul became ecstatic and started to make a marvellous build-up. His voice came out faintly into the hallway, and the employees of the firm stopped to listen to what was being told.

Nandi was convinced and still was not. He had a bunch of people here who were inefficient and wouldn't move an inch from their places. He wouldn't risk taking on board one more person and waste all the resources that were already being wasted. Upon all that, this boy was young and had no experience with offices at all. The tale of him being with the Sachdeva group seemed like it was worked on any way.

Nandi was at a very distressful position of his working life currently. He had fallen deep into the hole, and now he saw no way out of it. Only one instance of letting lose, and the entire system became flawed. Workers at the factory were at an unrest. Employees became a killjoy, and eventually it started to affect the workflow, which shattered the client base. The growing competition in the market would not be possible to keep up with. Since the work also went out of hand, the employees became more of a killjoy, and the situation at the factory grew graver every passing day; it was a paradox one could never get out of.

This process, as you can see, had sorely affected Nandi's state of mind. This paradox had taken in the boss too, which Nandi himself was somehow well aware of. So when Atul came in and did all the pep talk, his flow of mind did move from its previous place.

'Nice talking to you, big boy.' Nandi got up to shake his hand with Atul as he left the cabin. Atul was told that he'd be contacted back, but for that, he did not have any feelings. By the end of the meet, Atul was exhausted. He had spoken so much; in fact, at one point he felt as if he had spoken way too much to only make himself look like a whippersnapper.

Just as Atul came out in the hallway and walked up to the filter of water, then came Haider. Now you must pay close attention to Haider. With his long ruffled hair on his head, straight-fit and neatly ironed beige pants, and a sky-blue half-sleeved shirt, this chap didn't belong here.

'I heard your conversation.'

It was funny to Atul because he didn't remember the last time someone came up to him to say something, and this man looked like he was going to say something nice.

'Okay.' Atul almost flushed at the thought of it.

'He will hire you.'

Atul skipped a beat. Even if this weird guy wasn't the person to make the call, just to hear him say it made him feel like he had been waiting to listen to it for an eternity.

'Are you flushing, seriously? You look like a boy with talent. Why do you want to waste your time here though?'

'And why do you think I'm going to waste my time here?'

Haider rubbed his palm on his full face. 'Because you cannot change anything round here. Look around you. For how much time do you think these people are sitting here? They have all been here for a minimum of five years. Even older ones left with a worry of getting caught by anxiety. No one can change anything round here. If Nandi sir will hire you, he will only do so to satisfy his feeling of trying or giving another shot. This firm will shut down, and everyone will make better lives for themselves. Some might not. But why would you join and waste your time if eventually you will only leave?' Haider squeaked and hissed throughout.

Atul couldn't stop smiling. 'Okay, so you know so much about the state of this firm. In fact, you are in the phase of realisation and has very much accepted the truth. So why are you still here?'

Haider put himself to a mum. But he spoke moments later. 'Because I don't want to be remembered as someone who joined work and then left because it was at a bad stage. Every company has its low points, but if I leave at any one of these points, then I become a mean individual who wants to make good for himself but doesn't want to give back. And it will never stop. I will keep on changing workplaces because I will get into this habit of doing so. And then one day, one company will notice that trait in me, for which I will never be hired. Furthermore, when I look around, I get a good feeling because I somehow feel I am better than most of them.' He winked.

Atul waited for a moment and then raised his eyebrows at him as if telling Haider that if he was getting so much satisfaction in working here, then why should Atul stop himself from going ahead? 'And you have not even heard my story!'

By now, half of the office heard the conversation between Atul and Haider, and they were gaping at Haider.

Atul put his hands on Haider's shoulder and leaned in to whisper, 'By the way, if I get hired, let's sit over tea and discuss more things.'

Haider nodded in acceptance. 'And my name is Haider.'

They shook hands, and Atul remarked, 'And you can call me the smart one.'

Ten months later

PCM & Co. had been shifted to the first floor of the same building. It was a smaller office but was very warm. Some of the employees were shifted to other branches. Also, new ones were hired in this branch to match with specific skill sets. Staff was on the ground most of the time, and so it was a very busy day at work, entirely tiresome.

Atul was back at home. Yes, he did find a roommate, and with the salary he started to earn, it was possible to rent a house with another person. When Haider asked Atul about his address, Atul tried to ignore the topic for once, and later, Haider walked up to this cubicle and said, 'You know, my roommate has left for another city. So my flat is empty and can take one person. So before someone I don't prefer being my roommate asks me about joining, why don't you come on board? You know that I will never mind. Above all, the rent is fairly cheap.'

Atul smiled at him and hit him in the stomach then broke into laughter. 'Okay!'

'Okay then!' Haider whooped, and they did a quick hand hug.

No wonder Atul started to admire Haider at the first look.

After Atul received a confirmation call from Nandi, he rang Haider and caught up for some tea. It also was the day when it rained untimely due to the excessive heat from the past couple of weeks. So Atul had a one-in-a-million type of a day after he couldn't recall how many years. Making a friend in the strange city developed a feeling of warmth in him. Now that he came to think of it, not having someone to talk to or be physically in touch with made a lot of difference in his days of struggle.

He found a perfect complement in Haider. He was a nice man with broader than broad thoughts; his imaginations went way ahead of line, but he still managed to stay stuck on the ground. He was the kind who would rudely wake you up from your ever-long sleep to nothingness and who would pop the bubble in which you made yourself futile.

In fact, when Haider got to know about Simran and that Atul had been dealing so loosely with his relationship, he gave Atul an earful. 'Why would you do that with someone who has known you for your entire life? Getting involved in work is one thing, and getting so engrossed in your own world is another. Now that things have started to settle down in your own life, why don't you get back on track with her?' Sometimes Atul wanted to ask why Haider did not have a girl to himself but never found it correct to do so.

Haider was not just helpful in restoring Atul's personal life, but he was also a pro at work. Atul came up with plans, but to sit on everyone's head and overlook the projects was never done well by anybody but Haider. He knew which type of task to assign to which of the employees. He brought about the system of tracking and analysing the workflow of each employee, and since he was on his toes with everyone's job role and their achievements, a sense of accountability was brought in the office environment. Why Atul didn't put his hands in employee management was because he was aware of their distinctive hatred towards him. Atul did not have an ego about it but was more afraid to get into a brawl one day and disrupt the flow of performance. He was still to work on maintaining intimacy. During breaks, everyone did laugh at all his jokes, and during pressure of work, everyone did everything he asked them to do, but there was still a lot of tension in the atmosphere.

Things went off balance when one of the employees had so much frustration in himself that he not only resigned from the firm but also joined a competitor, disclosing all that Atul had worked hard on for the clients. The competitors made a better offer. It was at this point of time when PCM & Co. lost five clients in one go, which was a jolt for the firm.

But this technique from the opposition didn't work for long because four of the clients flew back in when they came to know that the functionalities of the other company were flawed and distorted.

You can always imitate, but there is a reason why imitation is called imitation.

This episode ushered in a lot of credence in the firm.

PCM & Co. had finally revamped and remoulded itself.

Ten months passed, and come what may, the situation at PCM & Co. only became better. On the tenth month, the firm got back its financial sustainability, the HR was in place, and there was absolutely no miscommunication in the flow and process of the work. Clients started to come back in, and so even the factory workers were settled because of the pile of orders coming in every day. Because of the upliftment of the overall scenario, Dev Nandi was a happy man, and because he was a happy man, PCM & Co. was a happy firm. Dev Nandi and his firm was in a paradox again. This paradox he never wanted to get out of.

12

The One with Deep Conversations

'Tell me, Atul,' Haider asked. It was night-time, and they were lying down on the terrace, on a folding bed they managed to bring up from their apartment. Atul was gaping at the dark blanket of the sky. For a very long time, he had not properly seen the night skies of the city, so now every time he takes a look at it, he is left amazed because of the vastness of it. The brawl was over. Was it real? Yes, the brawl was over.

'Atul?' Haider knew why Atul was gazing straight into the sky. 'Atul, the sky has nowhere to go. Now tell me. Would you choose money, or would you choose fame?'

Atul dropped his head to the side to face Haider. He squeezed his eyes and looked at Haider in a 'Have you lost it?' manner.

'Now, come on.' Haider pushed Atul's shoulders with his hand.

'Okay. I would choose fame.'

'I thought you'd choose money.'

'Don't you need money to get fame?'

'No. You can also do social work and earn nothing but still be famous.'

'I am the least likely to do social work. Some years back, I was the one for whom people would do social work!' They broke into fits.

Haider said, 'I'd choose money.'

'And that would be why?'

'Well, one reason being that I don't want any attention to my life. I want to live my life with money and do the things I always wanted to do. Getting fame involves people, and that makes you a socially bound person. Eventually, you become some sort of a societal psychopath.'

Atul couldn't understand. 'Okay, but don't you crave for love from people or the attention they give once you become something big and then what you do becomes a trend and people follow you and take inspiration from you?'

'Whoa!' Haider exclaimed. 'For what I know, you don't even take inspiration from other people.'

'That's not right. I don't make their motivation my motivation. How does anybody not take inspiration? I am not sure if a normal person is capable of doing so. We are getting inspired every minute of our lives.

'Yes, I don't blindly follow someone because today people pull out one incident from an inspirer's life and call it a path of wisdom one is walking on. But you don't even know what his life history was or what his future is.

'For example, if I get famous today, I will not want to motivate people to not study. They don't know what happened with me. Whatever choice I made was only a matter of personal choice. If a person living in the city decides not to go to school because I didn't go to a school, then chances are that he has taken the wrong motivation from me.

'I did not have many facilities in the village. My parents went through a really hard time, and whatever decision I made at that point of time is not something I would even like to preach.'

Haider now sat straight and looked back at Atul, who was still lying down, moving his hands in gestures and talking while facing the sky. Haider nodded.

'So, yes,' Atul added, 'I would choose fame.'

They spoke until midnight and then went downstairs to sleep.

13

The Offer of Promotion

The morning was very welcoming at PCM & Co. Nandi looked absolutely delighted, and it seemed like there was a new progress shown on the bar. Atul and Haider looked at each other and asked each other in their minds, *What is happening?*

Nandi took them by their shoulders and walked them into his cabin. 'Sit, kids. I have news for you!'

'Did Mukherjee call? Do we have their referrals on board?'

'Oh! Yes, yes. That happened the other night. Didn't I inform anyone?' Nandi looked at both of them, but they sat there, clueless. 'Never mind. We have clients coming in every week. It's normal now.' He laughed out loud.

Atul and Haider laughed along with him. 'Okay, you are very enthusiastic this morning. What is the whole deal?' Haider went ahead and asked.

'So we are arriving at the close of the year, and PCM & Co. has showed 150 per cent growth. It was something that was unimaginable only a year back.' Nandi pointed towards the event of Atul's arrival. Atul smiled from ear to ear as Haider did a small pat on his arm.

'The members are happy, and the clients are satisfied. We have taken ourselves from being insignificant to making a huge impact in the market—although the competitors are not in the best of their moods with the speed we have taken . . .' Nandi winked. 'We don't mind taking the risk to explore even more! Congratulations, children! Dated today, PCM & Co. is out of its debts and is taking a leap for making bigger profits.'

Haider's face went red. He felt his blood gushing through his body with excitement. There could not have been a better moment than this; he always wanted to see himself as a part of this company's growth, to once and for all stay at one place and not change his mind, to be consistent and witness development. This meant everything to him.

But just as Haider was going to believe that it was the only thing he wanted from life, Dev Nandi announced, 'And you boys are up for promotion!'

Atul and Haider sat frozen. They saw a good time coming, but to be up for promotion was insane. They were ecstatic and jumpy. Nandi had been a father figure, a shadow, and he had both of the boys' backs the entire time. PCM & Co. had become a family, and to get good news from family was a very emotional moment for all of them.

When the meeting was over, Atul pulled Haider to a corner. Haider got completely sentimental and hugged him and held him for a long time. But Atul was switched on.

Haider looked at Atul and asked, 'What? Are you not happy?'

Atul replied, 'Yes, I am. But can you stop being a girl and involve yourself in the conversation I am about to have with you?'

Haider was confused. 'Don't tell me you don't want the promotion because you are waiting for fame.'

'Don't kid around. Come, let's go for tea.'

Atul and Haider went back to the office after a long conversation. They directly went to the doorstep of Nandi, knocked, and peeped inside.

'Nandi sir, do you have a minute?' Atul asked.

'Yes, sure, come in. Is there a problem?'

'No. Well, actually, we had something to discuss with you which might just be too wrong or too right.'

14

The Midnight Slurries

1996

It was 12 a.m. And it was Atul's twenty-fourth birthday. His wife insisted on going for a fine dinner because, the following day, a very big celebration had been organised to welcome Atul's start of a new year and they wouldn't get any personal time to themselves.

Atul refused for once because his mind and body had gone for a toss, but he agreed when she insisted harder. 'There won't be any opportunity like today to let you know how special you are to me.'

She put on a long black dress which embellished her sleek body and left Atul wondering how she could look so perfect. He smiled at her and took her by the waist. They reached an exquisite restaurant where there was good music and delectable food. The wines came in. Initially, it was reminiscence to past years and how much fun it was during their days of childhood and what she thought of him throughout. When the mood set in, they went on to the bar, moving from the Lindeman's to Chivas. Drunkenness gave way to slurred conversation, and that was when honesty kicked in.

'You know, Simran, I did so much to reach where I am today. Never got a big jolt in the entire process, but right now, it feels like I cannot handle the stress. I forget I am just twenty-four—in fact, I just turned twenty-four! How much can one person even tackle?'

'But you are not alone. You have Haider, remember? You have Haider at least. But me, I have no one.'

Atul looked up to her and observed her for a minute, and when he kept on looking, consciousness made Simran break into shy giggles.

'What are you saying? I have given you a big house to live in. You can do all that you like to do—cook, dance, call friends, watch movies. And then these dresses! Look at you, you look stunning. What else do you want?'

'You. I don't have you. I am happy Papa and Mama are about to shift here. At least I'll not be as miserable as I am otherwise.'

Atul heard a notion of complaints coming out from Simran's mouth. He immediately felt unsettled but didn't react; instead he called for more drinks.

'When I meet Haider tomorrow, I will give him a tight hug. We have not been having a very good time at work.'

'Do you feel the same way about me?'

'What do you think I am doing?'

'Oh! So you are aware that we are not having a good time. And please don't say that you are trying to do something here. You turned down coming here in the first place.'

'But I am here.'

'Yes, now, after forcing you to do so. Why would you agree on second thought and not instantly?'

Atul got annoyed. He gulped the whole glass down to his throat and then dug his face on his arms resting on the bar table.

'Let's go.' He made a payment and got up. They silently waited for the car at the lobby, and during the ride back to their home, didn't utter a word.

Atul lay down on the bed in the same clothes; the annoyance turned into anger. But when Simran reached up to his chest to sleep close to him, he held her tightly.

After a few moments, she whispered, 'Happy birthday.'

There was no response. He had slept.

15

Mornings to Patch Up

Morning came, and before his eyes opened, he heard loud shouts of men saying, 'Junk reports! Junk reports! Junk reports!'

Atul sat up straight, unable to catch his breath. He put his face in his palms and told himself, *It's a new morning, it's a new morning.*

Simran was still sleeping. He looked at her and thought about the night, only to put himself in dismay.

It was his birthday, and he wouldn't let anything upset him today. There was a grand evening celebration which was waiting for him. Invitations had been sent to everyone from Dev Nandi's office to all his clients he met while working in the office and all the acquaintances he made along the way. The employees from the newest office have organised everything from food to music to drinks for everyone to get together and celebrate with them on the big occasion. It was going to bring new changes and a new year of life. Things would get better as they always did.

The doorbell rang. Atul took a moment to freshen up and went outside to see who has showed up. Sitting on the couch of the hall was Haider. He looked exactly the same man from three years ago—just with short hair and a clean-shaven face. He still had the same charm on his face, but the confidence of the man only grew to a level where someone would call him classy.

Atul had a shameful face and walked up to him as he opened his arms to embrace him.

'Well, happy birthday, young man. I bought you some flowers.' He made an awkward face, now thinking why he even brought flowers, if anything else!

'Thank you, man. You didn't have to.'

'Ah! Brother to brother,' he continued. 'So last night was a hell of a ride, eh?'

Atul was perplexed. How did Haider know about last night?

Haider started to laugh and said that Atul had called him sometime around four and told him the entire story at the restaurant.

Simran stood right at the door of her room and listened to everything they spoke about. She saw both of them laughing at the incident but made no expression when both the men saw her. She just raised her eyebrows and walked up to Atul to give him a kiss on the cheek and wish him a happy birthday. She then hugged Haider and greeted him a good morning.

'You guys talk while I prepare some breakfast.'

Haider got up. 'Oh, no, Simran. I will leave for the office now.' Then turning to Atul, he said, 'You stay back at home and don't come to the office today. Relax and come fresh at the party in evening.'

Haider left, leaving Atul and Simran alone. Just when Simran started to glare at him, he then rushed back into the bedroom, so Simran went into the kitchen.

You cant cross the sea merely by
standing and staring at the water.

16

The One with The Birthday "Bash"

The evening arrived, and Atul became anxious. He never thought that he'd ever be so frightened. His hands were shaking while dressing up. He couldn't stop himself from thinking what could happen. He might meet someone who would bring up the topic that was haunting him enough.

Simran walked into the room, wearing a satin gown with ornamented sleeves and neck. Her hair was done up into pretty locks in a bun, her eyes looked even more beautiful with the black lines that bordered them, and those red lips curved into the fullest of pairs. She stood at the back of him, and Atul saw her from the reflection of the mirror in front of him. He turned back to look at her, but when he saw the difference in her height, he looked down on her feet, and they both laughed. Simran ran her hands upwards on the black suit and reached to his forehead, held the sides in her palm, and pressed them together so as bring back Atul from his fears.

Atul opened her eyes and looked at her with a big smile. Everything was fine. Everything was going to be fine.

Atul entered the celebratory hall with an ear-to-ear grin on his face. He hugged everyone and spoke to everyone. There were people who were proud of him, like Dev Nandi.

'Look at you all grown up!' he said.

Then there were some of his colleagues from Nandi's firm who were pleased to see him. For them, it was like they were a part of Atul's progress from the plastic-bottle manufacturing firm to him building up something on his own.

For some other colleagues, all they could scorn about was the latest news of junk reports.

Initially, it was okay. He was able to tackle them with 'I know, what an unfortunate set of events!' But slowly, it started to take a toll on him. The clients started to mention it in a pitiful manner. The people he made contacts with didn't bother to keep themselves shut and made circles in every group and tell all of them about it. Gradually, the buzz started to increase in his own party.

He lost control and answered back a few with 'Hey, how old are you, and how much salary do you arrive at in each month anyway?' or a 'Yes, I am also twenty-four, and I have earned more money than what you will in thirty years to come'.

Haider watched him from a distance all this while. He was observing the downright attitude of Atul's in his own party with his own guests. He went up to him and realised that Atul was drunk out of his heads.

'Hey! What do you think you are doing, brother?' Haider asked nicely, holding Atul by his armpit.

Atul looked up and gasped, 'Haider! My brother! Hey, guys.' He turned to the audience. 'Hey, people!' He clinked his glass. 'This is Haider, my friend, my brother, and my business partner. He is the best man I have ever come across, way better than all you minute pieces of nothing!'

Haider got flushed with embarrassment and looked for Simran for some support. Simran broke in and announced, 'Okay, everyone, thanks for showing up today, and thank you for being a part of my husband's special day. Atul will now take off. Please, you all enjoy the evening. Food and drinks have just started.' 'Thanks, all!' Atul exclaimed and strode outside the hall into his car. Simran went away with him, while Haider attended to all the guests.

Aim for the moon. If you miss, you may hit a star.

17

Mornings That Falls Apart

Another morning arrived, and when Atul woke up, he made sure he banged his head into the bed. He slapped himself, cursing, 'Shit, shit, shit, shit!'

Simran stepped out of the washroom after taking a bath and started putting her clothes in a suitcase. 'I am going to my mummy's house, and I don't know when I will return.'

'What? Why?'

Simran stopped and turned to him to as if start shouting. 'Because'—then she took a pause to cool down—'I cannot either argue with you or support you while you go everywhere, getting drunk and creating a scene.'

'Hey!' Atul retorted.

'No, don't act like you are offended because I have been taking loads of silent offenses every single day! Listen, there's no point of a discussion. Your clothes are out, go and get dressed. You are late for the office. Drop me on your way.'

Atul kept silent. He went to take a bath, and when he came outside, he saw a reflection in the mirror of a man he recognised from the past. He met this man some four years ago—the same small but wide saggy eyes, long thin legs, but no tan on his hands this time. His hair was still messy, and what was underneath would yet again not be seen once he wore his clothes—a peach shirt and grey trousers.

18

So What Actually Happened?

Everything was meant to change when, some three years ago, Atul and Haider walked into Dev Nandi's cabin. The next day was the first day of the business calendar, and all the employees of the firm were accumulated at one place. Dev Nandi ran through the progress statistics of the firm, and everyone roared into applause. It was a day of celebration for everyone because their hard work had paid off.

But there was one announcement left to be made. This brought chills to Nandi's spines. 'As you know, the overall upliftment of the firm from one platform to a notch higher and to five notches higher, they were from the major hands of two kids who have proved to be victorious today. I will come clean and let you all know that the other day I ushered them into my office to give them a promotion.' Everyone gaped. They knew what was coming up. 'But they refused promotion.' Perplexity took over. 'Instead, they offered to contribute in another way. They proposed to hold equity shares in PCM & Co.' There was silence in the room. This was getting interesting for Dev Nandi. 'And they now hold equity shares in our company.'

The whole staff was awestruck. Nandi reached to both of them and hugged them. Everyone else started to hug both the boys.

It was a start of new beginnings for them. They loved the attention, and then, working hard was never a problem for them. Years passed by, and now, in fact, they had enough free time to themselves. Atul got a new phone, and he started to make calls to his home. It felt good to be back in touch with all his loved ones.

One day, Atul was speaking to his mother while having breakfast. He was getting late, but he thought that he could speak since she called. But later he thought it was not a good idea after all because she told him that Simran's parents were waiting for a call from their side and asked whether she should say yes for starting the preparations for their wedding.

That day, Atul was late for work.

Everything took place too fast, and it felt as if just overnight Atul had his wedding and then he was found handling his marriage.

When the money started to flow in, there was no time to even think about the marriage. Both men left no opportunity to learn more and more, and meeting more people was always a great feeling. They had their aim set. They were to start something of their own now. Two more years passed away in the blink of an eye.

The market knew about the talent that this two possessed. These boys had also let the word out that they if any company needed any consultancy services, they would be up for it. So when a company contacted Haider for an R & D project, Atul was on cloud nine.

At first, they themselves initiated the project, but when work pressure took over, Atul had a plan. He always had a plan.

'Why not outsource our project to Dheera from the office?'

'What? Are you insane? It is our first project, and you want to outsource it?'

'Yes, why not? Think about it. The expenses will be worth it. Just see the amount of money they are going to pay us for this project.'

'Not happening. We cannot just let someone, anyone, do the project.'

'Haider, you know there is a lot of work pressure at the moment. And on top of it, we have officially accepted the project. Now do you want to miss a deadline and create an ill impression?'

Haider rolled his eyes in dismissal.

Atul reassured him, 'We'll supervise it, so don't worry.'

But management was at its worst peak. Atul could not keep track of the project timelines, and the day of submitting the R & D had arrived. Atul asked Dheera again and again if everything was in place or not, and Dheera assured him that they would like the project.

Two days later, response for the company came in. The mail read, 'Junk report.'

19

This One's Going to Bring Them Down

Haider's eyes were stuck at the screen. Atul couldn't believe himself. This was going to bring them down. Haider took chances and called the director of the company, only to hear even more disheartening statements from him: 'Useless report', 'Inability to do business', 'We have nothing with you any more'. And it went on and on.

Both the boys were in a state of shock. The regret was not of losing the project but of losing their relationship with the client. This meant that sorting out further business for four other cities went for a toss. Their reputation built on goodwill for four years was destroyed in minutes.

Within a matter of ten days, the news spread in the entire market, which eventually seeped into the personal life of Atul, making him miserable yet again.

If you can dream it, you can do it.

20

But There Comes Another Invitation

When Atul reached the office, Haider was already sitting on his desk. He smiled back, which put off Atul.

This is going to be another sarcastic set of lecture, he thought to himself.

'Yesterday was . . .' Haider got up to speak.

'Is it necessary?'

'Okay. But yesterday—'

'Oh god, Haider! Is it really necessary? I know that things went wrong but—'

'Yes, it did go wrong. But then it also went right.'

Atul stopped to look at Haider. 'What?'

'Yes, we have received another R & D project from Gupta.'

Atul took a deep breath and fell on his chair. Haider leaned down to him and whispered, 'So you want to outsource it?'

21

The Separation

After the drunken scene at Atul's birthday party, Mr Gupta had approached Haider, saying, 'Failure has taken a toll on him. I know you guys closely, and I know exactly what you both must be going through. Look, if you want to seriously get into this business, then I am ready to give you another chance.'

The messed-up celebration brought in Mr Gupta, who gave them another chance, but Atul didn't know if he would ever get a second chance from his wife. Marriage had put Atul in a complicated direction in life. As much as he hated to admit it, before his marriage, he just had one focus, but after his marriage, everything looked dishevelled. He loved Simran when she was back at the village. He loved her when he was in the city and wanted a personal touch of life, for which Simran was always there to speak to him.

But time passed by, and the feeling of making life bigger and bigger ate up Atul's mind. But when it came to hurting someone, he was not sure if he was still in the right direction. Maybe dealing with business was easier for him than dealing with emotions. After a long day from work, his brains wouldn't work in the right manner. To take along another person in a struggling life was never easy.

He still thought he would talk it out when she came back. He would put in another effort, extra effort. These were strictly prescribed by Haider.

After two weeks of her non-existence from home, a post arrived at Atul's house. She had sent her divorce papers. Atul didn't react but just made it look like she was just angry. Once they talked, everything would be fine. But the calls were painful. She spoke about all the frustration she had for two years, even more than that. She said that she married him not to be disrespected and thrown away as garbage. Each night, every night would be about another argument, which about how Simran caved herself. She wouldn't have to spend nights on cold beds, where there was no warmth from her husband. She would not have to wait for him to come back home for hours and hours. She didn't have to fight with him and act like a big support in his life because she knew she never was one. She was just a trash can that was used to spit in. Maybe she was a pillar, 'but now the pillar has fallen, and the whole building has collapsed'.

They were now separated.

The goal is to die with memories, not dreams.

22

If You Want to Become Anything, Then Become Modest

Atul numbed himself to emotions. He started to get fully involved in work. The new business also needed the attention. Atul worked day and night to work on projects and planning. By the end of the year, they had together completed thirty projects, and now it was time to set up an office of their own, which also meant they could start hiring. It also meant that now it was time to name their business consultancy firm: Padrea.

The name Padrea was not a spontaneous decision. Atul and Haider had dreamt of this name day in and day out. They knew it would be the correct name. *Padrea* was a combined word made from two separate, really close words to both men, *passion* and *dreams*.

There were heaps of talented people who would have loved to come on board to form a team. There were some really honest people these men met throughout their journey, and they knew they had to get those people on board.

The interviews started, and Atul and Haider were pretty much blown away by the kind of interviews that took place. Atul always recalled his interviews. They were sickening to the stomach. He was thrown out of a lot of places due to many reasons, and what happened at Sachdeva group was unforgettable. For the experiences he had, he wanted to make everything correct by giving the best of interview times to both the eligible and non-eligible.

Haider noticed the change of behaviour in Atul. If there was one thing he had become, then it was modest. Haider never saw this side of Atul. But he knew what Atul was up to. He wanted to give everyone an experience, and he knew that meant a lot to a struggling journey. Now that Atul had most of the better life to himself, he wanted to use the power to never let anyone have an ill experience—at least intentionally.

23

The Long Road: The Cost of Ambition

It was a long road for Atul. He met every kind of people—from someone like the boy who asked him to vacate his apartment to someone like Haider, who gave him shelter; from someone like Mishraji, who never let him have a hard time at work, to someone like the ones who kicked him out of the interviews; from someone like his father and Dev Nandi to someone like Kunal Sachdeva.

He faced obstacles everywhere, be it the boys in the village who never wanted Atul to strike the right place in *kancha* or the first project disaster for R & D.

But his faith was restored by many angelic people in his life; we know about them all.

By the age of thirty, his entire consultancy firm was in place, and it became a nationally recognised company.

In between, he did meet some old people, like Mr Kunal Sachdeva, who was now old but still stood upright and handsome. He started to wear suits of other colours. When Atul spotted him in a party which was organised for social welfare, he didn't hesitate to approach him. Kunal Sachdeva looked at him with an unbelievable gaze and did a handshake. Atul was happy to meet him too because he felt that this life wouldn't have been possible if not for the things he went through with Sachdeva.

Later in the same party, he spotted Simran with her husband, a business tycoon in the metal industry. They exchanged eye contact but didn't speak a word.

By forty, Haider had taken his share of money and quit Padrea to travel alone and witness jaw-dropping beauties of life. Atul laughed at him initially, but then he let him go because that was what Haider wanted since the very beginning. He had left his marks at places, and now it was time for him to take off and lead a life with the money he earned by himself. It was always money and not fame for him.

24

Never Stop: The Final Refection

2016

Today, the business had expanded to more than just India. Padrea was now a well-known business consultancy firm.

Atul Kumar had to fly to Singapore this evening, and so he was waiting for the plane, sitting at the airport. This was unsettling for the man who was sitting right beside Atul Kumar. He had been chatting with him for over half an hour now, and he had known everything about his life history and how he made a life of his own.

He asked, 'You are multimillionaire today. You own a private plane. The car which will take you to the plane will come to you, and it can come to you whenever you want. Then why have you been sitting here, waiting?'

Just as the man's question was completed, a black S-Class arrived. Atul smiled and got up. 'Nice talking to you.' They did a handshake.

While Atul walked towards the car, the man shouted from the back and asked another question, 'In fact, you should be having men to start businesses for you. Then why are you going all the way to start something new?'

Atul stopped and turned back to the man, still smiling. 'Tell me, what have we learnt? Is there an end to learning? And is there an end to achieving?' Turning back around, he went inside the car, while the man stood there, amazed.

Atul got down from the car to board the plane, but in the middle of the way, he saw a child. He started to call out for someone to check on the child, but then the child turned towards Atul and asked him to walk further. Atul knew who that kid was. He knew those small wide eyes. The eyes were grey, but when they were exposed to sunlight, they shone a hue of brown within.

He started to walk up the stairs, and even the child went along with him. The door closed behind them.

Printed in the United States
By Bookmasters